Zombie Mombie

Saves the Day

Written by Kelly Lucero   Illustrated by A.J. Lucero

Five AM alarm beep beeps.
Zombie Mombie wakes from sleep.

Eyes half drawn, it's only dawn.
Zombie Mombie stifles yawn.

Zombie Mombie breathes a sigh.
Dawn's upon, time to fly.

Slippers drag across the floor.
Zombie Mombie opens door.

Zombie Mombie sees the stairs.
Toy jeep catches her unaware.

Stumble, trip, and then—oh no!
Zombie Mombie bumps down low.

Coffee brews and starts to drip.
Zombie Mombie takes a sip.

Relax and read; the coffee's great!
Zombie Mombie can't be late.

Now up she gets the lunches to pack.
Zombie Mombie don't forget the snack!

She gathers speed, no lead in step.
Zombie Mombie regains her pep!

Up the stairs as quick as you please.
wake zombie babies from their Zzz's.

Brush the teeth, grab the clothes,
Zombie children come to blows.

Tumble, bumble down the stairs
Zombie kids with teddy bears.

Food is cooking, clanging dishes.
Zombie Mombie gives good wishes.

Dressed and fed with bags all packed
Zombies load the van in back.

On the road, the clan keeps going.
Zombie van, with lights' a-glowing.

Now it stops at Zombie school.
Zombie Mombie keeps her cool.

Zombie children wave goodbye.
Zombie Mombie heaves a sigh!

Honk, honk, beep, beep.
Zombie Mombie schedules to keep.

Zombie Mombie phone's a ringing.
Bad news 'bout her children bringing.

Dash to school, no time to waste.
Zombie Mombie makes great haste.

Zombie family to the clinic dash
then off to fill a script with cash.

Zombie Mombie goes to the store.
Kids complain, it's such a bore!

Zombie Mombie's shopping list
starts with cheese and pretzel twists.

Zombie Mombie's ready for lunch.
She buys some carrots by the bunch.

Zombie Mombie back in the car.
Time for pick up, school's not far.

Mothers line up in a hurry.
Kids come out of school and scurry.

Home again to homework blitz
while Zombie Mombie cooks some grits.

Zombie children take a bath.
Zombie Mombie has a laugh.

Read a book, play a game,
Goodnight wishes on Zombie train.

Creep and crawl back out the door
While Zombie children beg for more.

Blow last kiss then fall to the floor-

Zombie Mombie trips once more.

Zombie Mombie end of day.
Babies sleep the night away.

About Atmosphere Press

Atmosphere Press is an independent, full-service publisher for excellent books in all genres and for all audiences. Learn more about what we do at atmospherepress.com.

We encourage you to check out some of Atmosphere's latest releases, which are available at Amazon.com and via order from your local bookstore:

The King's Drapes, a children's book by Jocelyn Tambascio

Beau Wants to Know, a children's book by Brian Sullivan

Young Yogi and the Mind Monsters, a children's book by Sonja Radvila

Buried Treasure, a children's book by Anne Krebbs

The Magpie and The Turtle, a Native American-inspired folk tale by Timothy Yeahquo, Jr.

The Alligator Wrestler: A Girls Can Do Anything Book, by Carmen Petro

My WILD First Day of School, a children's book by Dennis Mathew

I Will Love You Forever and Always, a children's book by Sarah M. Thomas Mariano

The Sky Belongs to the Dreamers, a children's book by J.P. Hostetler

Shooting Stars: A Girls Can Do Anything Book, by Carmen Petro

Carpenters and Catapults: A Girls Can Do Anything Book, by Carmen Petro

Gone Fishing: A Girls Can Do Anything Book, by Carmen Petro

Owlfred the Owl Learns to Fly, a children's book by Caleb Foster

Bello the Cello, a children's book by Dennis Mathew

That Scarlett Bacon, a children's book by Mark Johnson

About the Author

Army wife and experienced juggler of time, Kelly Lucero and her family of five currently reside stateside in Florida. With a background in Elementary Education and a master's degree in Reading & Literacy, Kelly is a current Educational Consultant. With over 20 years experience working with children, she has a knack for creating meaningful stories to share with young readers and their families. Consider visiting her author page focused on creative learning solutions called KellyLucero.com.

About the Illustrator

Audrey resides in the Keweenaw Peninsula of Michigan, with her husband, son and daughter, and a guppy. When not in mom mode, she does painting, drawing, reading and listening to music at a high volume.

CPSIA information can be obtained
at www.ICGtesting.com
Printed in the USA
LVHW071625190221
679378LV00015B/184

9 781636 495538